To my husband Bob for his love and encouragement and to my children Eric, Amanda, and Ashley for going along with their mom's ideas.

www.mascotbooks.com

Do You Like White Steak?

For more information, please contact:
Mascot Books
620 Herndon Parkway, Suite 320
Herndon, VA 20170
info@mascotbooks.com

Library of Congress Control Number: 2019910853

CPSIA Code: PRT0919A
ISBN-13: 978-1-64307-426-9

Printed in the United States

Do You Like White Steak?

Valerie Barlow

Illustrated by Vanessa Alexandre

Mom was in the kitchen. It was early in the day, but my brother, sister, and I were wondering what Mom was making for dinner.

When we asked her, Mom replied, "White steak."

We had had steak before, but not **white steak.**
Hmm. What did that mean?

As we played outside, we kept thinking about **white steak**.

We saw our mailman come down the street, so we ran up to him to ask if he knew what it was.

"Excuse me, Mr. Mailman. Do you know what **white steak** is?"

He looked confused.
"No, sorry!"

We thanked him as he walked down the street, but we still didn't know what **white steak** was!

We played some more and noticed our neighbor walking her dog. We decided to ask her if she knew what **white steak** was.

"Hi Charlotte," we said.

"Do you know what **white steak** is?"

She smiled and said, "No, sorry!"

It was getting closer to dinner and we still didn't know what **white steak** was.

Then we saw Dad come home.

"Hi Dad! Do you know what **white steak** is?"

He laughed. "Yes, I do! Follow me."

We followed Dad into the house
and sat down at the dinner table.
Mom put a piece of **white steak**
on each of our plates.

It looked like steak.

It was white and crispy all over,
but it smelled really good!

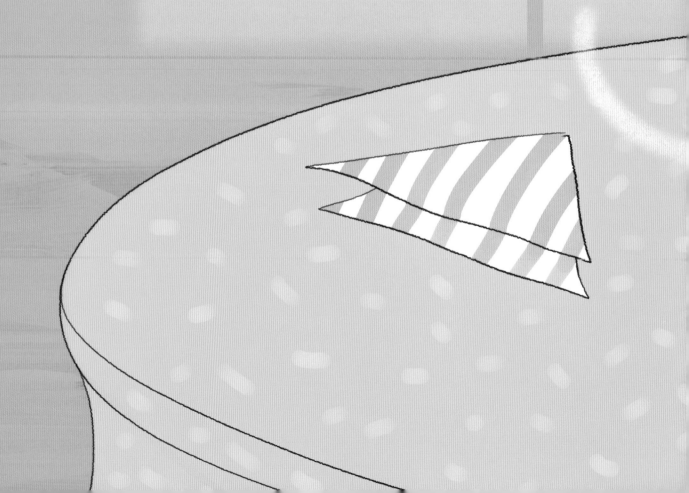

"Maybe we should try it," we said.

It was delicious!

Mom asked, "Do you like white steak?"

Recipes

I wanted to include a couple of recipes that I use when I cook for my children. I know many parents that have had a hard time getting their kids to try new foods, and the technique that I share in this book has worked on my family for many years.

While steak is beef, **white steak** is another name for pork chops with the bone still in. Here are some recipes utilizing "white steak" in delicious ways - from my home to yours!

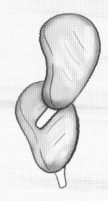

Cream of Mushroom White Steak

6 bone in pork chops (white steak)

1 can of cream of mushroom soup or can of cream of mushroom soup with garlic

1 can of water

1. Line pan with aluminum foil.
2. Place pork chops (white steak) in pan.
3. Pour cream of mushroom soup over pork chops.
4. Add 1 can of water to pan and mix with cream of mushroom soup.
5. Place in oven at 350 degrees for 1 hour.

Tip: Great with mashed potatoes or rice!

Barbecue White Steak

6 pork chops (white steak)

Barbecue sauce or soy sauce

1. Grill pork chops on grill. It will give lines like a barbecue steak.
2. Spread barbecue sauce or soy sauce on pork chops before removing from grill.

About the Author

Valerie Barlow was born and raised in Massachusetts, where she later graduated from Holyoke Community College. She moved to Florida in 1985 and has remained there with her family for over 30 years.

Valerie has recently retired from the medical field and school lunch service so she now travels the country with her husband of over 40 years, Bob, in their RV. Valerie also enjoys making crafts and paddleboarding in her spare time. She has three married children and four grandchildren.

Do You Like White Steak? is Valerie's first children's book.